T0197514

Issue #1

"The Warning"

TRIPLE
AAA
ALIEN, ALLIENCE, AGENCY

Created By
DEION TILLETT

Copyright © 2021 by Deion Tillett. 836129

All rights reserved. No part of this book may
be reproduced or transmitted in any form or by
any means, electronic or mechanical, including
photocopying, recording, or by any information storage
and retrieval system, without permission in writing from
the copyright owner.

This is a work of fiction. Names, characters,
places and incidents either are the product of the
author's imagination or are used fictitiously, and any
resemblance to any actual persons, living or dead,
events, or locales is entirely coincidental.

To order additional copies of this book, contact:
Xlibris
844-714-8691
www.Xlibris.com
Orders@Xlibris.com

ISBN: Softcover   978-1-6641-9648-3
        EBook   978-1-6641-9647-6

Print information available on the last page

Rev. date: 10/22/2021

LATER...

HUH!? W-WHERE AM I?!

CALM DOWN...

YOU'RE IN TRIPLE A HEADQUARTERS.

WE'VE GOT QUESTIONS FOR YOU.

NO NEED. I WAS SENT TO GIVE YOU A MESSAGE FROM YOUR FORMER AGENT.

UH OK...

I DON'T REALLY REMEMBER ALL THE DETAILS. BUT THIS I DO KNOW.

I WAS IMPRISONED ON A BOUNTY HUNTER SHIP. AGENT CARLOS, AS YOU SHOULD KNOW WAS ON A SECRET MISSION.

WE WERE BOTH UNDERCOVER TO INVESTIGATE A RISING TYRANT.

WE WERE SUPPOSE TO COME BACK HERE AND WARN THE AGENCY. WARN YOU THAT HIS NEXT TARGET IS EARTH.

BUT...

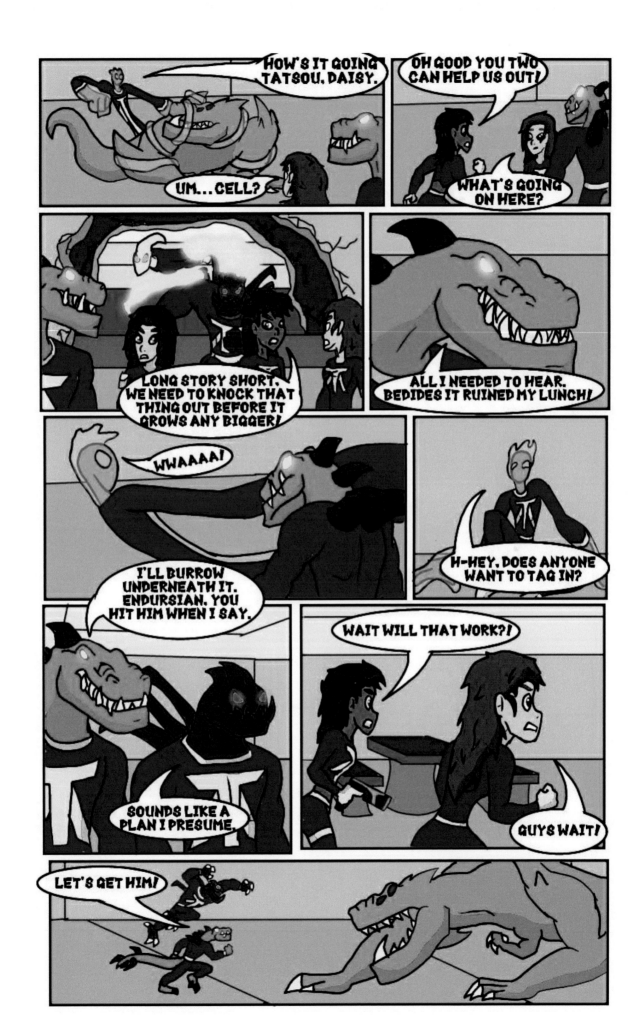

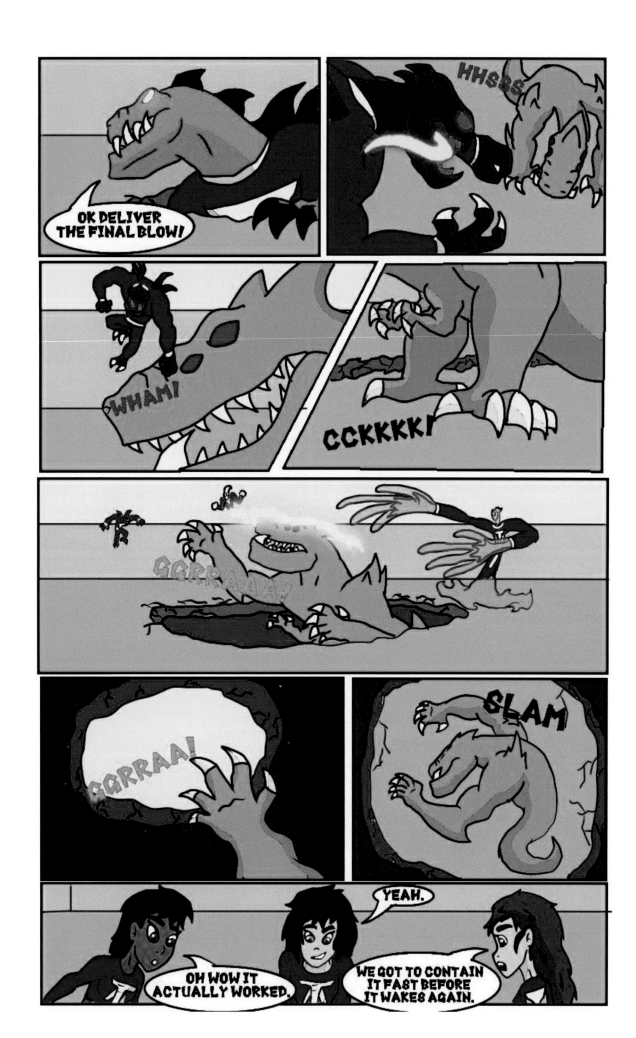

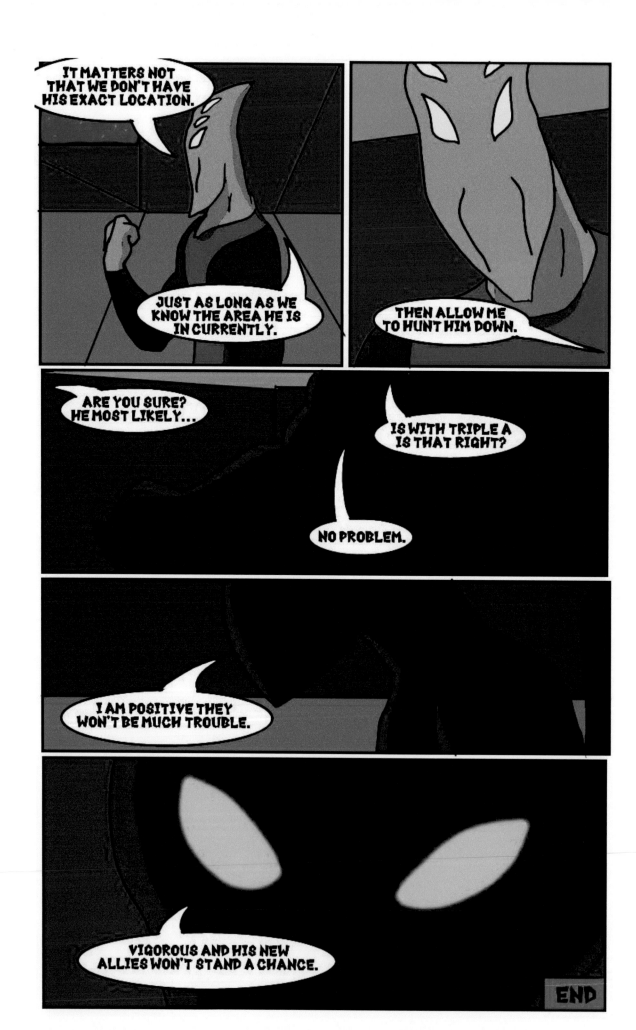

Printed in the United States
by Baker & Taylor Publisher Services